THE NORMAL HEART

Madelon Sprengnether Gohlke

Madelon Sprengnether Gohlke

THE NORMAL HEART

Drawings by C. D. O'Hare

The Minnesota Voices Project #4

New Rivers Press

1981

Copyright © 1981 by Madelon Sprengnether Gohlke
Library of Congress Catalog Card Number: 81-8379
ISBN: 0-89823-027-6
All Rights Reserved
Typesetting: Peregrine Cold Type
Book Design: C. W. Truesdale

Acknowledgements:
Some of these poems originally appeared in the following
publications: *Fallout*, *Lake Street Review*, *The Little Magazine*,
and *The Real World*. Our Thanks to the editors of these magazines
for permission to reprint.

This book was published with the aid of grants from Dayton
Hudson Foundation, Jerome Foundation, the Arts Development
Fund, and the National Endowment for the Arts. This publication
was also made possible by a grant provided by the Metropolitan
Council from funds appropriated to the Minnesota State Arts
Board by the Minnesota State Legislature.

The Minnesota Voices Project books are distributed by:

Bookslinger,
330 East 9th St.
St. Paul, MN 55101

and

Small Press Distribution, Inc.
1784 Shattuck Ave.
Berkeley, CA 94709

THE NORMAL HEART has been manufactured in the United
States of America for New Rivers Press, Inc. (C. W. Truesdale,
Editor/Publisher), 1602 Selby Avenue, St. Paul, Minnesota 55104
in a first edition of 1000 copies, of which 25 have been signed and
numbered by the author and the artist.

For Crescentia Phillips Sprengnether

THE NORMAL HEART

I

II

III

IV

I

SUMMER 1976

"I hid from the curse
Like a goddess
Who has lost her power
To keep life alive."
                    May Sarton,
            "Learning About Water"

This dryness, the days
like diamonds, a rain of sun
like stones, each day
a bird fallen from the sky
snake coiled in the water pump
dead in its own labyrinth
water
runs under snow, mounting
to a ringing in the ears
at the dip in the road
the tipped cup of the uterus
raining blood, this
our loss, our responsibility
this knowledge
of small things dying
a woman's story.

OKLAHOMA

By late June
the leaves have darkened
and glitter like locusts.
The earth is sore
and always has been.
The sky like a small blade
scrapes it clean of children.
The road is heavy with slow-moving vehicles
cement trucks, air-stream trailers
and an occasional harvester.
Too much ice water
makes me nauseous
the odor of beef lots
unrefined oil and mimosa.
It is 53 miles to Wheeler
a town of burning corrugated tin.
By the side of the road
urging us on is mile after mile
of shining barbed wire.

IT'S COOL OUTSIDE AND BRIGHT

It's cool outside and bright.
People are playing tennis.
But here on the double-decker metal bed
it's hot. I'm wet. I'm not strong enough.
Bruises are flooding to my skin
on my arms, my legs, my neck.
He thinks I'm hysterical, but I can't scream.
I can hardly even talk.
"Please take me home, please, please."
I'm a virgin. I have never known pain.
But I'm not. Look, I'll unbutton my blouse.
you can touch my breasts and my hips.
I am a witch enchanted into youth.
You are the first. I'm the king's daughter.
Do something for me. I will make you rich.
He sweats like a bull, but I'm too simple
too American. I wear myself
like a wrap-around skirt.
We ate breakfast this morning
at the Pancake House. Not here.
I don't belong in this country of eagles and snakes
where the sun comes crashing down like an axe
and the sea vomits.

TIME AND SPACE EXHIBIT, MPLS. PUBLIC LIBRARY

The sun like a mother draws us to her.
Spinning in a long elipse, we turn
away to freeze, toward to burn,
intolerably cold or warm
bound to something we cannot directly name
without becoming blind
or looking into shadow
the metaphysical blaze of Henry Vaughn
God's skirts, like a sunflower,
drawing us deeper into danger.
But we have never been able to avoid
the center, the black hole
furious and invisible
that waits in space, unblinking pupil
the raving darkness from which we came
and into which we shall return
consuming and consumed.

PHOTOGRAPH: BREAKFAST, TRAIL'S END RESTAURANT, KANAB, UTAH

The milk is preternaturally
white, the cantaloupe
scooped and halved
as open and warm as a woman.
The napkin lies demurely folded
under the fork while a spume of butter sinks
into a short stack of pancakes.
This is the land of molten copper and salt.
Dreaming we drive through the heat and flats
impelled to whatever end
we have forgotten, but here our last meal
may be what we came for, hoping,
as after death, to meet someone,
a wish as alive and clear
as the spoon crossed casually
over the stainless steel knife.

THE MAGIC FLUTE

They believe in pictures.
Isn't that how it always begins.
He falls in love with her portrait,
gold hair, rose and white skin,
supplied by her mother who grieves
some loss inconsolable.
Queen of the night she cries
stunningly for death.
She is dizzy with the idea of it.
It rocks her like a baby to sleep.
Her daughter, however, must refuse
the knife. She and her lover
must walk through fire
on a sinuous line of music
the phantom hope
of Papageno's bells, Tamino's flute.

THE ANDES SURVIVORS

They had no interest in sex
their genitals shrunk to a wart
dry and fevered while all their blood
rushed to the mouth.
They gave their bodies to one another
in death, consuming each organ,
lungs, liver, small intestines,
brains, and heart, bone to marrow,
flesh of one flesh.
Eating, they discovered,
is the greatest pleasure,
imagining banquets, seven course dinners,
the specialty of each house
as they gnawed on a hand
or a strip of fat.
The females, of course, they saved for last,
sister and mother, the old taboos
sacred before God, high
in a cordillera
of the Andes, as they dreamed
each night in the months before Christmas
of the Blessed Virgin
who never ate anything, holding an orange
or a pomegranate, extending her nipple
to the insatiable baby
in her lap.

TO GIOTTO

The angels are in agony
in your viscous sky
dwarves in nightgowns
with gold plates on their heads.
They wring their hands.
They twist and turn
suspended over the human pain
on the ground. There Mary Magdalen
a foot fetishist to the end
weeps over his toes.
His apostles, his friends,
uncertain how to respond,
stand back with hands folded.
What is there to say?
It is the mother who makes them feel
unwanted. She strains anxiously
for any sign
over the long white body
of her son.

TO ANNE SEXTON

Woman I never met
whose poems I have read in class
would recommend to friends
not enough like Sylvia Plath I said
to gas herself
father-lover, daughter-hater,
mother-killer, hung up on Christ
and holy babies you can eat
I didn't expect
you to die, the suicide in you
something you'd accept like a guardian angel
following you at a respectful distance
but not ever want to talk to
all night in your automobile
as if you were going somewhere
dressed up and carrying a silver
cigarette case.

WALLY'S SONG

Washing in the blood
washing in the blood
washing in the blood of the lamb.
It's not red and it's not real
it never gives birth
and it's not menstrual.
It doesn't clot and it doesn't kill
it won't wear black and it's not
unfaithful
and it binds itself willingly
like any young animal.
It longs for the knife
and it comes to your call
and it takes, it takes, it takes away all
the lust and the guilt and the shame.

YOUR MEDIUM IS WATER

Your medium is water
because it has weight
because it has mass.
In the greenish light, behind glass
you can see the large fish
and the marvellous plants.
A diver with a movie light
attached to his mask
would look for the archaic
and the grotesque.
But beneath your Pacific, the ocean plates
are wrinkled
bearing the creases of struggle
and at that depth there is no light.
What lives and moves in the dark
is known by no one and the language there
like the songs of the narwhale
piercing and rudimentary
is full of pain, full of labor.

THE TRAIN IS SILVER

The train is silver, noiseless
shining diesel, going west
and you are young, half-way to California
after Christmas; you know that because
there are cards all over in the snow
after the accident and you pick one up
to read it, the only things intact
these messages, except for the baby
which has turned blue and puffed up
like a balloon from internal bleeding
and doesn't cry which you think
must be a bad sign.
The husband you can see was killed instantly
while the woman has a cut on her neck
so you put your hand in and pinch the artery
thinking someone, maybe you, should stop this.
Her skirt is torn off and she is wearing
yellow panties. The car was dark blue
the sky is light, and the train is silver
moving slowly backwards.

THEY CRY BADLY ALONG A ROSE

In March, the sky unblooms
like an old guilt.
We avoid it as we avoid turning back
into a room that is empty.
Hardy kept throwing his dog a stick
until he swam too far out;
he wanted to see him disappear.
The snow looks like rocks with holes in it,
like dirty coral,
like hard ugly sponges
with eye sockets.
In spring, at this time of year,
we cry badly, a woman standing in the doorway
bleeding from all her pores.

THE PERSISTENCE OF
THE UNCONSCIOUS IN THE LETTER

Hysteria, the language of the body
having its revenge
raging, sobbing, pleading
for understanding.

Paranoia, the real world
of unreality, where nothing means
what it seems to. My brother,
standing in the doorway
saying, "I don't trust mother
and I'm not even sure
I trust you."

Hand-wringer, foot-tapper
the compulsive, making lists
keeping meticulous tabs
on chaos.

Oh, somewhere there is a child
crying, in a dream, closeted, mad,
a holy ghost who comes in fire
to speak with our tongue.

TO YOU SIGMUND FREUD

Not as the floors of a house divide
the basement from the kitchen
waking from sleeping
air from water.

We can't make it better.
The seaweed, the rotting fish
we drag up won't be prettier
in the living room dried
or pried loose from its flesh.
The smooth bone will stink
whatever we do to it, here
or on the beach.
We can stand at the edge of our continent
watching it come in
the ocean's pleasure inumaginable to us
our backs to the fire, faces to the cold
foam rising in the night
but we can't take it back.

Eyes will never turn to pearls.
Coral can't be made from bone.
Words, like everything else,
decompose.

If it works it is because
we submit ourselves without wishing
without crossing our fingers
or making signs to it
as my daughter watches
a man eviscerate a baby trout
its small heart as desperate as her own thoughts.
Because in her mind
it is always taking place
just as it was
the slippery things inside the fish

turning into trash
the jumping heart inert,
its rapid and surprising blood
turning her green life red.

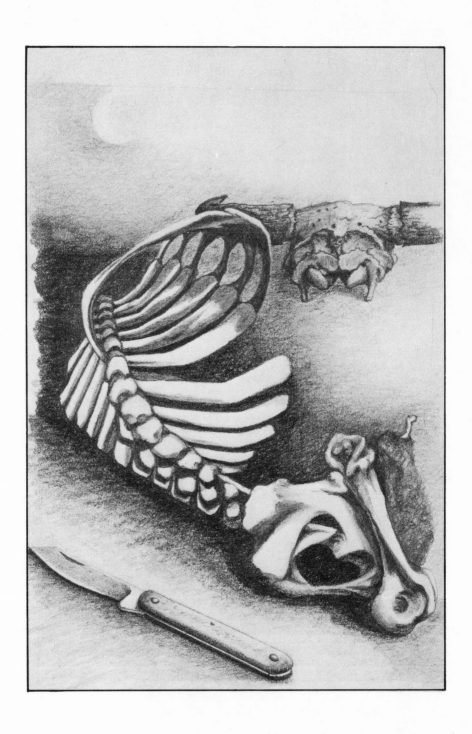

II

JEHOVAH'S WITNESS

Sunday morning, she is intent,
a small woman with bouffant hair,
and a listless ten-year-old daughter.
She fixes me, a few inches
from my cautiously cracked screen door,
with her gaze. "My life," she says
"was meaningless. We are born,
we die, and what for?"
The day is clear and warm.
I stand in the doorway, unable
to say no, unable
to meet her eyes, dark
with anxiety. Her voice
as she reads from a book
called *The Truth That Leads to Eternal Life*
is oddly soothing.
She says she will return
(though she never does)
to discuss the Bible with me.
In heaven, she reassures me, as she goes,
there is comfort
and someone who will wipe the tears
forever from our eyes.

TEARS IN THE ALBRIGHT KNOX

In the gallery of the blind I hear them saying
that the sighted are no different.
I have trouble leaving this exhibit.
Later, when you ask, I tell you how I hated
being different as a child, how sick I was
and how miraculously I survived
through penicillin. And then you remind me
of how your mother died at twenty seven
from the same illness. That evening
at dinner, over wine, you say
that sitting on the bench
in front of Jackson Pollack you were crying
and that you wanted me to notice.

THE BOOK OF RUTH

When Naomi lost her two sons
she wore her memory
like wreaths of dead hair
nursed her emptiness like a baby.
Orpah kissed her and went home to her mother
but her daughter-in-law Ruth
wouldn't leave her. "I can love you
better than they," she said,
"wherever you go, I will go, your people
will be my people."

Ruth was a gleaner. Sorrow had taught her
how to regard the earth.
When the gaudy man Boaz
took an eye to her
Naomi told her what to do.
"He is an uneasy sleeper.
Lie at his feet, and in the morning
he will fill your cloak
with barley."

It was all true.
Boaz wanted her more than money,
more than oil or spices.
Her suffering relieved him.
She was his ballast, her firm belly
his clue, his answer.
But when the baby was born
Ruth returned to Naomi;
"here is your son, nurse him,"
she said. "Wherever you go he will go
his people will be your people."

J'AMY, JULIA, PAULA, AND KIM

The names of women, the names of girls
clipped or romantic
whisper to one another
a dialect: I might have been Jules
or Paul or James were it not for a slur
of the tongue, like summer,
a relenting.

The subtraction of syllables
makes Kim
in her new body, who will never marry
she says, her father so perfect
so handsome.
J'Amy, the elder daughter is shy,
her eyes half-closed, her smooth legs
burnished like wood. Julia, the clown,
sees vaginal openings in every design
protects her white skin, makes naked women
in bronze. Every day she arrives
like some fairy godmother
with good things to cook. Paula will only laugh
sometimes; curious and amused
she walks like a boy, sketching in her mind
the drawings she will never show, secure
in her household, she could go
for a walk in the neighborhood
and never return.

Girls become women; this my own daughter
will deny though she knows.
It's not so different
I try to tell her, our secrets are open
and closed, our lives entwined
like the vibrations of sound that shiver along
our garlanded names.

ANTONY IN DRAG

You like the tight soft dress
so different from the cool breastplate
that does not caress your chest
the way this violet Egyptian silk
does. The delicate pins
and the smoothness of your skin
felt through the fine cloth
excite you. You want to touch her
almost as a woman would.
Your arching penis is not a sword
but something pliant like the snakes
she loves and winds you with.
When she comes, guiding you
with her hips and legs
you know that Venus is a god
as great as Mars and for a moment
in the gaudy bed, in the mass
of perfumed, multicolored scarves
you cannot tell your arms,
your hands, your mouth, your hair
or your white thighs from hers.

GLASS WALKER

Like a man in mourning
he is careless
of their expectation
naked in his blue sweat suit
with feet as innocent
as babies.
He is listening
for a sound as thin as blood
while inwardly he treads
on locusts, darkening
before him.
The path to the American
audience is twenty
seconds long, and now
he can see them
at the edge of his shadow
their pink tongues
and bright red hearts
like rows of cotton candy
their palms sticky
with spun glass.

PERRY SMITH, *IN COLD BLOOD*

Not eating like that for days
makes you think of your mother
the blue behind her head
when she laughed
dirty clothes in the room
where she slept
your sister falling over and over
like an acrobat
from the eighteenth floor
your other sister, pretending
like an Avon lady
to be normal
your legs breaking like matchsticks
under your motorcycle
the girl saying "Please don't, no"
hiding her gold watch, like Cinderella,
in her slipper
the father whose throat you cut
the son whose head you wanted
to obliterate, like all thought
of the woman at the end of the hall
who waited, quietly,
for your bloody footsteps.

NEWSPAPER STORY

"Be thus when thou art dead, and I will kill thee
And love thee after."
                              Othello

He hits her with a hammer.
He has been thinking about this
for years, detailing
her infidelities.
Not with men; the way she cheated
the government, for instance,
not charging any sales tax,
running too much hot water,
leaving food on the plate.
She always indulged herself.
Now he sees her sleeping
like a child grown into the body
of his grandmother,
a woman who has lain beside him
cool and dry for thirty three years
untouched.
He will make her bleed, he thinks
not asking her permission
first the head
and then the cunt.

AUGUST

Month of recurring storms, like dreams,
of children, bored by play, who break their toys,
of unexpected drownings at the lake
of the long sun that has lost the will
to move, month of refusal
like an angry clitoris beaten to a rage.

Lie still.

That God will come we know from the intermittent
flashes and the heat
to relieve our desires
to relieve us of ourselves
(like fish panicked in a bowl)
to take us, like the world, and eat.

THE DREAM OF COMFORT

The dream of comfort dies.
The seamless body of the child
is fissured, cross-crossed with hurt
by the time it learns to speak, to walk.
There is no party line.
We live from our immensities
always, feeling the pressure
of our selves, the voice that cries
from our tissues and organs
that grieves in words too simple
for us.
I would like to say this
some other way.
My daughter cannot be sure
there is any such person
as God or the devil but she thinks
there must be a Jesus.
While abstract good and evil
are beyond her imagination
her small faith fastens
on the mystery of pain.

The Seam of Things

splits. We wanted so badly
to be normal. Money
helps. Death is so easy
coming on us like something familiar
a hamburger stand
a Walt Disney movie.
Saturday morning bursts
with a phone call,
like a medicine chest full of pills,
the commitment to difficulty
cutting like glass on a hand pushed
through a locked door..
It hurts like a tube
shoved down the throat.
We take up positions
around this new event
holding grief like an unlooked for gift
too expensive to unwrap.

I, Pierre Riviere, . . .

Hiding from the act, I sought
for a month, feeding on roots, no flesh
though I knew how to hunt and trap
small animals, squirrels, rabbits
I had flayed and crucified with nails
and sticks, simplicity in nakedness
walking the roads openly at midday
with my sword.

Better I knew than anyone
the nature of suffering, the cry
of creatures broken beyond recognition
pleading for death. Deliverance is the only gift
we have from God who cuts us
like a boy beating cabbages with a stick.

As long as I could I worked
to understand the divine anagram
"calibene"
something beautiful, something good
lying dark in a word
sometimes a weapon
sometimes pure invention.

We bear, always , more than we can.
I sharpened my bill, laid out
my dark suit, the color of night
and slaughtered first
my mother who was cooking
my sister who ran
screaming into the yard and my brother
who was innocent.

I wore for a while their blood
on my hands, proudly, like a woman.
What was bright in them I released like a flame.
But slowly, my body, like a bruise,
blackened from within. What is animal
is foul. Only the bones are clean.

Language is a fury that will not leave me.
Sleep is a drug made of anger and pain.
Time is a knife hurled without mercy.
A haste, a haste I have for the end.

THE DEAD TORMENT US

The dead torment us.
They grieve us like hunger.
They bite us like cold.
Calling to us
from their featureless landscape
they pull at our hands
like children.

We must
break their legs
gouge their eyes
strip the skin from the head
and wear a finger bone.

They are full of envy and malice.
They want
our lives.

III

FOR MURIEL, WIFE OF

The lives of women must be
a carefully guarded secret
and you are glad
in these public dances
like the precise steps
of a wedding march, the turn
at the right place, the look
on his face, surprize
even then
the words formal
a life shaped in the eyes
of others, that your grief exists
in a way that can be
documented
leaving you the luxury
you have always had
of crying
when the children
have all gone to bed.

FOR ESTHER

Though I usually buy lightbulbs
75 watts, five year guarantee,
from the organization for the handicapped
this time I buy knives.
This time
instead of getting off the phone
with a quick order, I listen
to how your husband left you six months
after cancer, one breast with glands,
and you had a no good lawyer
who didn't know how to protect you
how another customer lost her husband
to a twenty-three-year-old
couldn't hardly wait to get married
the day after the divorce was final
how you've had the flu all week
can't get to the office even
how you called the wrong number
reached my husband who said
we don't live together
and your voice, always familiar,
tells me "Honey, believe me,
I know just what you're going through,
believe me, I've been there,"
and you begin to describe
your excellent kitchen products,
your dishcloths, your floorwax,
your detergents, your brooms,
and then the singular virtues
of your beautiful, infallible knives.

HEMORRHAGE

(for Joanne)

When you exercise you begin to lose weight
but your body needs its cushions of flesh
like peaches.
At seventeen you stood in the kitchen
and started to bleed from the neck to the waist
bruising
in a minute.
Holding your death now inside you
like something precious
you keep reminding yourself
not to break.

THIS IS FOR MOTHERS

This is for mothers who find their sons
dead for no reason they can understand
in their own homes on a cold
November morning, after breakfast
going down to do the laundry
in the basement.
He took the rifle he had used
all last week hunting pheasant
with a friend, silent, so that everyone
thought he was O.K., thinking about going
back to school, wanting to see
his longtime girlfriend, hoping
this time it would be better.
She wanted him dressed well
clean and neat, his hair trimmed
his skull closed, the blood washed
from his eyes, so that everyone could tell
that he was all right
the way she had made him
that she had nothing to do with this
shattering.

THE SIEGE OF LENINGRAD

What we see, steadily,
through the flickering of 1941
to 1943 are the hands of women
touching, smoothing, caressing
straightening a collar
bending the already stiffening arm
their faces covered by scarves
tied behind, bodies dark
and lumpish in the cold
while their hands perform
a necessary labor.
This is what it means to be
at war.
The men, with some deep intent,
are hurting each other
while the women
with cries like winter birds
open their plain, bare hands
to mourn.

THE CONDITION OF TRANSPARENCE, READING LACAN

(for Claudia)

Everything for the paranoid
has significance, a bell ringing,
the look of a stranger, a conversation
in the dark. The paradox of mistrust:
in a world full of accident
knowing your place. When you are twelve
or fourteen in the French Alps
living with Nazi sympathizers
and carrying false papers, your parents
already pegged as Jews
and you see a woman shot in the head
from your bedroom window, so close
that you observe her blood,
it is better to believe in election or damnation
than to abide by the useless spectacle
of pain.

NOSFERATU

(after Werner Herzog)

The blood knot ripens
in summer,
frothing on her lips.
She believes
that blood is holy.

Pale, pale, without reflection,
he grows pale
from unbelief.

October opens its throat.

Drunk with darkness
he will leave her
crazed by wolves
her flesh as white
as snow.

AFTER SURGERY

blood every day
like rain
each afternoon
the slow seeping

the jellied clot, soft but firm
rolled between my fingers

the bunching of a small balloon
like bubble gum, breaking
between my legs
arterial splurge
from my real heart
muscle that confesses
my sex, its pulse
accelerating my life
into the already
oxygen rich
air

childlike
so magnanimous

ILSE

The light from the television screen
at 3:00 a.m. in Abbott Northwestern
hospital is restless,
murmuring. Ilse, your voice
behind the canvas curtain:
breast biopsy, frozen section,
something to estrange
the pain. Your life
in Germany before the divorce,
the IUD that made you bleed
on your friend's car seat,
the history of migraine,
the onset of menstruation at nine,
your chemistry
strung on birth control pills
and ergotamine. You pull
the curtain, your face fuzzy
and we agree that the emergency
room is dangerous, your undiagnosed
skin disease, the deadly staph,
my bleeding, and now like Penelope
in the dark heart of mercy
we are impatient to undo
our histories
our words shuttling faster
towards the syllables of silence
the other babel of our dreams.

GENIE

Your father and brother
barked and growled:
this is not a metaphor.
When they looked at you
they saw a dog.

For eleven years
they kept you harnessed to a chair.
Was it a smell of blood
which alarmed your mother
into thinking
you were something like herself?

Your father, seeing horror
in the mirror of authority,
killed himself
a distinctly human act.

When you wept you made no sound
while your captors
a group of linguists
overflowed with noise.

The grammar of your universe:
chair, window, sky, dish.
At eighteen there are things
you understand but will not say.
And when there is something
new you want to learn
you begin with the sign
you have chosen to let them know this.
Pointing, with the urgency to name
rising in your throat,
the sound you make is
"Hurt."

KAREN

Because she loved him
Because he said he'd kill her
Because of the children
Because she believed him

Every day he beat her
as a pastime, from boredom
because it was natural
because she was a bad housekeeper
because he needed her

He hit her for being in pain
throughout her labor
then helped her deliver
She didn't know who
had the right
She left him but
he knew her number
Like an obscene phone call
"Baby, baby come home"

That night he told her
he was tired, asked her
to wait, while he rested
too weak to hold
the metal studded belt
by now there were five guns
in the house

She shot him once in the shoulder
because he said he'd kill her
and again in the stomach
because she believed him
and three times in the air
because of the children

and in the chest because by then
he was quiet
because she didn't know who
was holding the gun
because he was still breathing
and because she loved him

THE NORMAL HEART

Born with one two-chambered
heart, the infant boys
died within days.
These children who could not bear
to grow apart
in the primitive confusion
of their valves
shared everything that mattered,
breath, blood, heat.
It wasn't that they didn't want
their mother, whose flesh harbored
their intimacy but that
there was no room for her.
Her ordinary love, which spewed itself
all over the delivery room
severing herself from herself
for their first gulp
of her own oxygenated element
was too bloody and complicated
for this pair
joined in a fierce and lasting
embrace.

FOR BECKY, WAKING UP

I was there. I saw your pain
those first jostlings of your sleep-
turned brain, the subtle break
of ice on water numbed
by the slow beating heart
of winter.

Like a child you took to sleep
so that you wouldn't break
the tension of a life numbed
by its first fall, like the heart
exposed to winter
or awakened to the sight of pain.

Broken, we prayed for you to break
again, the numbed
silence, the refusal of a heart
to mourn its winter
to know the darkness and the pain
of this blood-filled sleep.

We held our hands numbed
to the small fire of your heart
your winter, our winter,
speaking quietly to your pain
calling to something deeper than your sleep
to rise, like the sun, and break.

Was it our own heart
we feared lost in winter
our own blood stopped, no pain,
the careless traveller who sleeps
in snow, one who breaks
to another realm, breathless, numbed?

Month after month of winter
lies around us; to feel the pain
this seamless sleep
must break
the brain cells, bloody, numbed,
must take their hurt to heart.

Becky, such sleep is pain.
To live, you knew you had to break
the heart of winter.

IV

I DREAM OF GOLD IN A TIME OF PAIN

"Those joys were so small that they passed unnoticed,
like gold in sand, and at bad moments she could see
nothing but the pain, nothing but sand; but there were
good moments too when she saw nothing but the joy,
nothing but gold."

Anna Karenina

Driving into the canyon
in the late afternoon
and it begins to rain.
A rush of water to the left
flashing
lucid.

Dolly, careworn mother
of six children one dead
in her pink coffin
is shocked by Anna's revelation
about contraception.
In this nineteenth century
bulwark against change
women must count their children
like guineas.

My woman friend sundered
by her mother's madness
talks softly of the filament
of her awareness, tracing
the crescent shaped scar
on her wrist.

Women of our time
we share confidences:
one child, an abortion,
our fierceness

towards one another
driving into the canyon
our eyes on the river
searching, as the first prospectors,
who named the *Cache la Poudre*,
for the fine gleam of gold.

THE BADLANDS, DRIVING WEST

Malpais, mauvaises terres
for the pioneers bad to cross
an interim, not a stop.
We stop, a man, a woman and a child
in the summer of 1981 on our jagged route
west and south. In our sedan
we carry food and water
and it is not too hot, but outside
it is dry with glare
and things crumble under our feet.
I have wanted color, but all I see
are pinkish patches where the hills
have scraped their skin. Sometimes
a fillet of bones will emerge
from the layers of clay and ash.
This is a graveyard
for creatures unlike us:
camels, three-toed horses, titanotheres,
oreodonts, and sabre-toothed cats.
In the Visitor Center there is a display
of Indian artifacts. Not much can live here
they say, still some things survive
like the yucca and the rattlesnake
on the ravaged slopes. I don't know
what it would take to give back
what was lost when the White River withdrew
the bison died and the marsh dried up
but the National Park wants it this way
to remind us of our past.
Mako sica the Arikara called it.

LUPIN, NATURIST CAMP

The body I have lived in
for 39 years feels rumpled and worn
like slept-in sheets.
Around my swimming suit I am brown
and look good, I think, but underneath
what I have tried to conceal is spongy
and white.
The young girls so coolly nude
are playing volleyball, stretching themselves
like cats. No one notices here
they say: it is not erotic.
If one man's penis is dark and hangs to the side
I might see this as a camera
keeping my focus in a light flicker
not wanting to be rude
as I size this place up; checking the sling
of an abdomen, the curve of a buttock
the lift of a breast.
Where do I fit? I keep rubbing
oil into my skin, touching myself over and over
my thin hands warming to the sun's
small flatteries. The water when I swim
shocks me with its long liquid embrace.
I begin to appreciate the luxury of hair
and line, the intimate articulations
of bone, the lavish praise of flesh.
But naked, it is a young boy
who startles me by his grace
with his smooth body, his small sex
tucked into his groin—as quickly
and carelessly he folds himself
into his father's arms.

MESA VERDE

How can we know them
the Anasazi—Navaho
for the ancient ones

who labored out of the earth
led by Spider Grandmother
toward the sipapu

the heart-hole
to this long green table
its breast bared to the sky

these basketmakers, builders
Pueblo, whose kivas contained
a secret passage for the soul

who abandoned their houses of sun-
struck adobe, for the peach-carved
sandstone cliffs, for the peril

of descent and the climb
a people who loved the idea of edge
the sharp light of the canyon

who lived, worked
and vanished
from their open honeycomb.

THE CANYON AT 4 P.M.

Boredom in the canyon, a little rain,
no sun. I know that I am eating too much
drinking too much, waiting for dusk.
I run, for the first time in weeks,
my heart loud and grabby,
anxious in the elbows and knees.
Under the railroad bridge in black
spray paint, the Savage Skulls Rule.
Climbing, determined to climb
this new hill with its gold
dust, its ochre on the road
that clings to my shoes
I see foxtail as sharp
and light as your hair
fluted flowers
lavender, white.
And green so intense in fat leaves
I don't believe it has been there
for days, and my breath that hurts
is bright, is bright, is bright.

LA JOLLA

What are these flowers crowding me
over the walk, pink and cupped
like a hand, the hot night hugging me
in its sticky arms, the stars
exposing themselves overhead?
On the beach I am amazed
that I have come to the end
of this country jammed
with cars and color T.V.
Neon lights make the beach fires
flare like Blake's tiger,
the waves aggressively white.
They come towards us like tongues
frothing with saliva, the moon falling heavily
towards the oblivious earth.

PINK SKY IN SAN JOSE

Pink sky in San Jose then
lemon colored, straw colored hills
like apricots
like soft bread rising and folded over
like bellies, breasts and thighs,
the wheat colored grass cut in swirls
and swathes against these close-sheared animals.

This is orange, plum, tomato
country and garlic.

I could cup my hand over it
as I smooth the crease between your buttocks,
thinking of something like hibiscus
like peach
thinking of Celso
and his Brazilian carnivals, the men
sashaying like women, the brilliants
raining down bodies for days
and the jungle where you might sit
on a tree trunk that was in fact
an anaconda
gleaming yellow
that could eat a pig or a baby
and sees everything, even at night
with its bulging eyes.

I DREAM OF ST. LOUIS
FROM CALIFORNIA

In my dream the house is shut up
on Accomac street, my old neighborhood,
covered with plywood,
the whole front yard brown and flat.
To the side of the house though
in the kitchen window I see a woman ironing
and the back yard gate,
as it used to be, unlatched.
The bed of iris is there and the breathless roses
the tiger lillies rampant against the back fence—
the worn spots under the swing set
where we scuffled our feet.
I could leave this yard some afternoon
my pinafore starched and cool
over my bare shoulder blades
my feet in white sandals stencilled
with stars, my hair curling
from the heat.
I could skip down the sidewalk
to the soft heartbeat
of summer and the murmur
of sprinklers scattering light sorrows
into the grass.

PORTRAIT

Your bathroom is the color
of lime sherbet
or the icing on a child's
birthday cake.

The frame on the mirror
like porcelain is white
the tiles in the shower
a deeper green.

How could this be like
a forest, or moss, or simply your back yard?

Should it matter that the french doors
in the bedroom open out to a balcony
and the plain light of the street?

That your plum tree, overgrown,
is tangling with fruit,
your petunias as dark and simple
as a Georgia O'Keeffe.

IN THE COUNTRY

The house moves towards me in the dark
present, physical,
each room pulsing a peculiar light
lemon, lime, peach,
each holding me
in its illusion.

Men inhabit trees, wolves,
the fire with its mouth
spewing the universe
in a trail of coals.

We cross the fire
on a wave of flame.

Men and women stand
as if at the end of the world
gathering themselves
back into their bodies
like divers springing
back to the board
sparklers returning
to the fuse
a waterfall
a rose.

The tomatoes, unstaked,
lie with their warm skins
next to the earth.

I walk into the house like a painter
my hands speaking to the lines
of the wall, lending themselves
to my designs. In the morning

I will rise
I will sweep the floor
I will pour the milk
into glasses with marigolds on them.

Madelon Sprengnether Gohlke